ARCHIE'S
HOLIDAY

for

Charlie

x

Bloomsbury Publishing, London, New Delhi, New York and Sydney

First published in Great Britain in 2013 by Bloomsbury Publishing Plc
50 Bedford Square, London, WC1B 3DP

Text and illustrations copyright © Domenica More Gordon 2013
The moral right of the author/illustrator has been asserted

A CIP catalogue record for this book is available from the British Library

ISBN 978 1 4088 2932 5

1 3 5 7 9 10 8 6 4 2

Printed in China by C & C Offset Printing Co Ltd, Shenzhen, Guangdong

All papers used by Bloomsbury Publishing are natural, recyclable products
made from wood grown in well-managed forests. The manufacturing processes
conform to the environmental regulations of the country of origin

www.bloomsbury.com
www.domenicamoregordon.com

ARCHIE'S
HOLIDAY

Domenica More Gordon

BLOOMSBURY

LONDON   NEW DELHI   NEW YORK   SYDNEY

HAIL?
RAIN? SNOW?
HURRICANES?
LIGHTNING?
THUNDER?
WATERPROO
LONG, THICK, WOOLL
MORE SOCKS!
YIKES!
FREEZIN
NO!

EVERYTHING

OCKS

YES!

Ahhh!

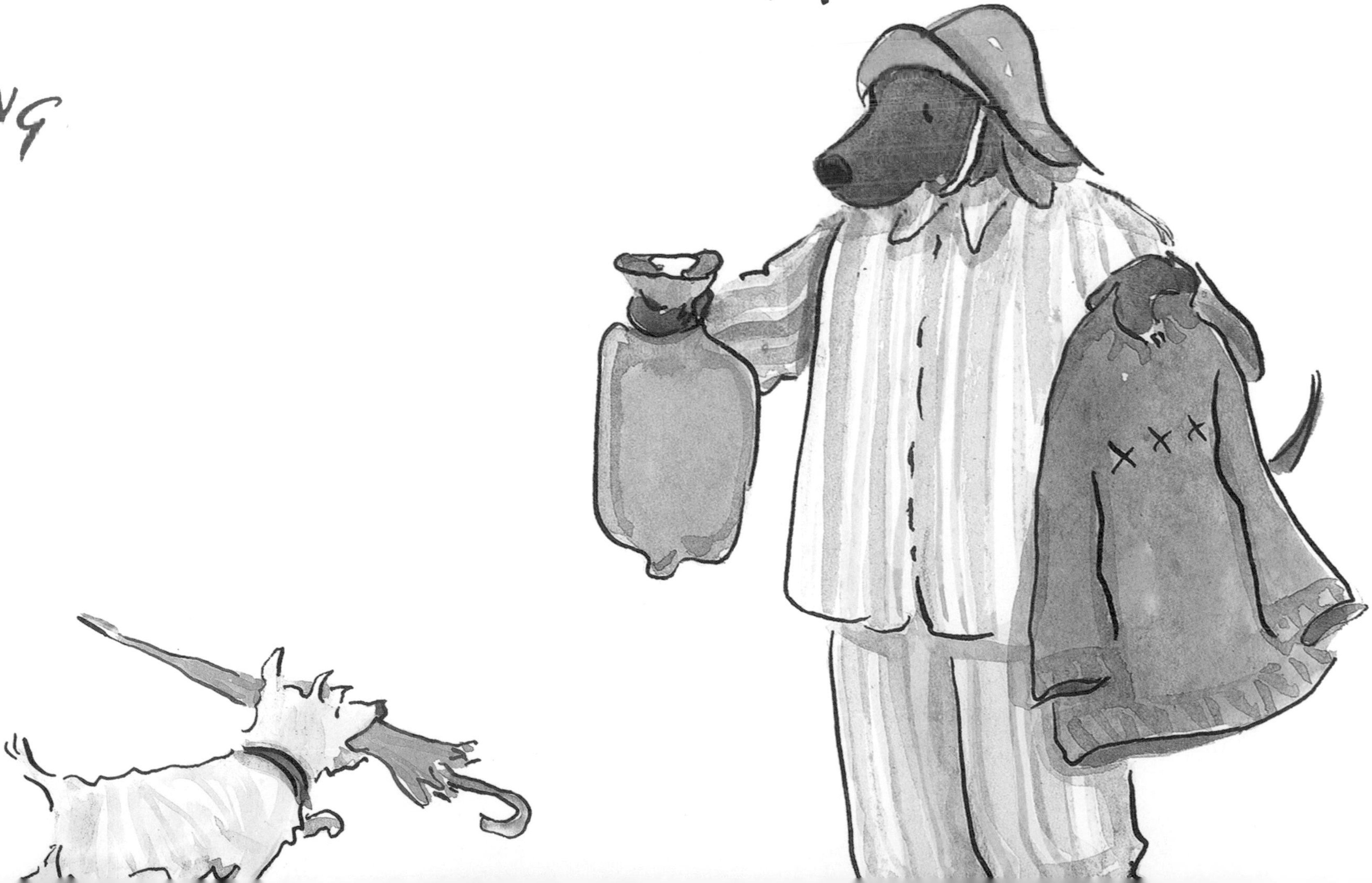

PILLS FOR EVERYTHING!

BLUE PILLS, RED PILLS, LOZENGES

ALL POSSIBLE TYPES OF CREAM!

JELLY FISH STING CREAM

SMALL PILLS

BIG PILLS

ICE PACKS

ANTI SNAKE VENOM STUFF

MORE CREAM

PHEW!

ALLERGIES?

HELP!

THAT'S BETTER!

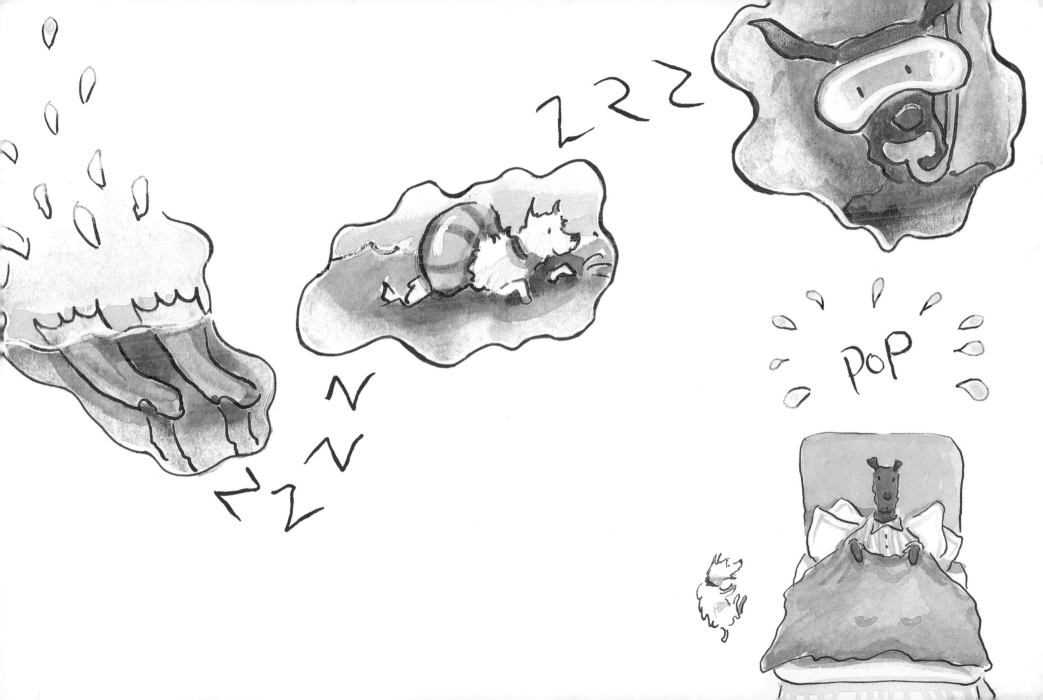

DECKCHAIRS x 2

BLOW UP LOCH NESS MONSTER

SHARK CAGE!

SPADE

FRYING PAN

ARMBANDS Su

SWIMMING CAPS + 2

WETSUITS

PIRATE

? BAT

SHARK

EXTRA TRUNKS

SUBMARINE?

WINDSURFER ? BAT

SU

'THE WONDERFUL WORLD OF SHELLS'

WINDBREAKE

FAKE SHARK FIN

BARBEQUE BUCKET

'KNOW YOUR SEAWEED' BOOK

BEACH BAG

CANOE?

CRICKET BAT

SNORKELS + 2

FISHIN

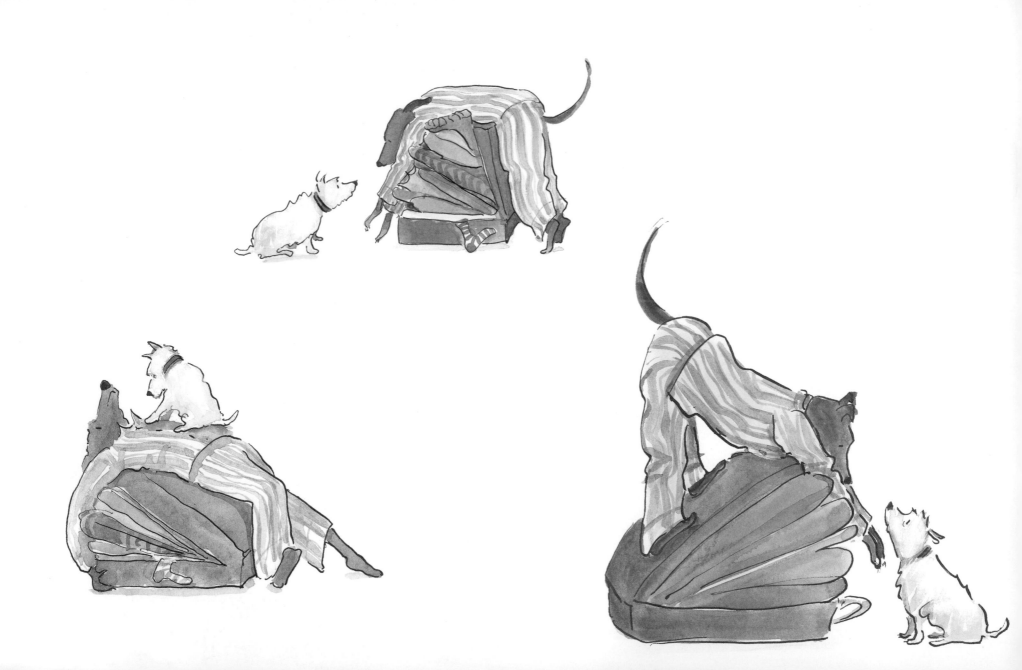

BA

CREEEAK

BARK
BARK
BARK

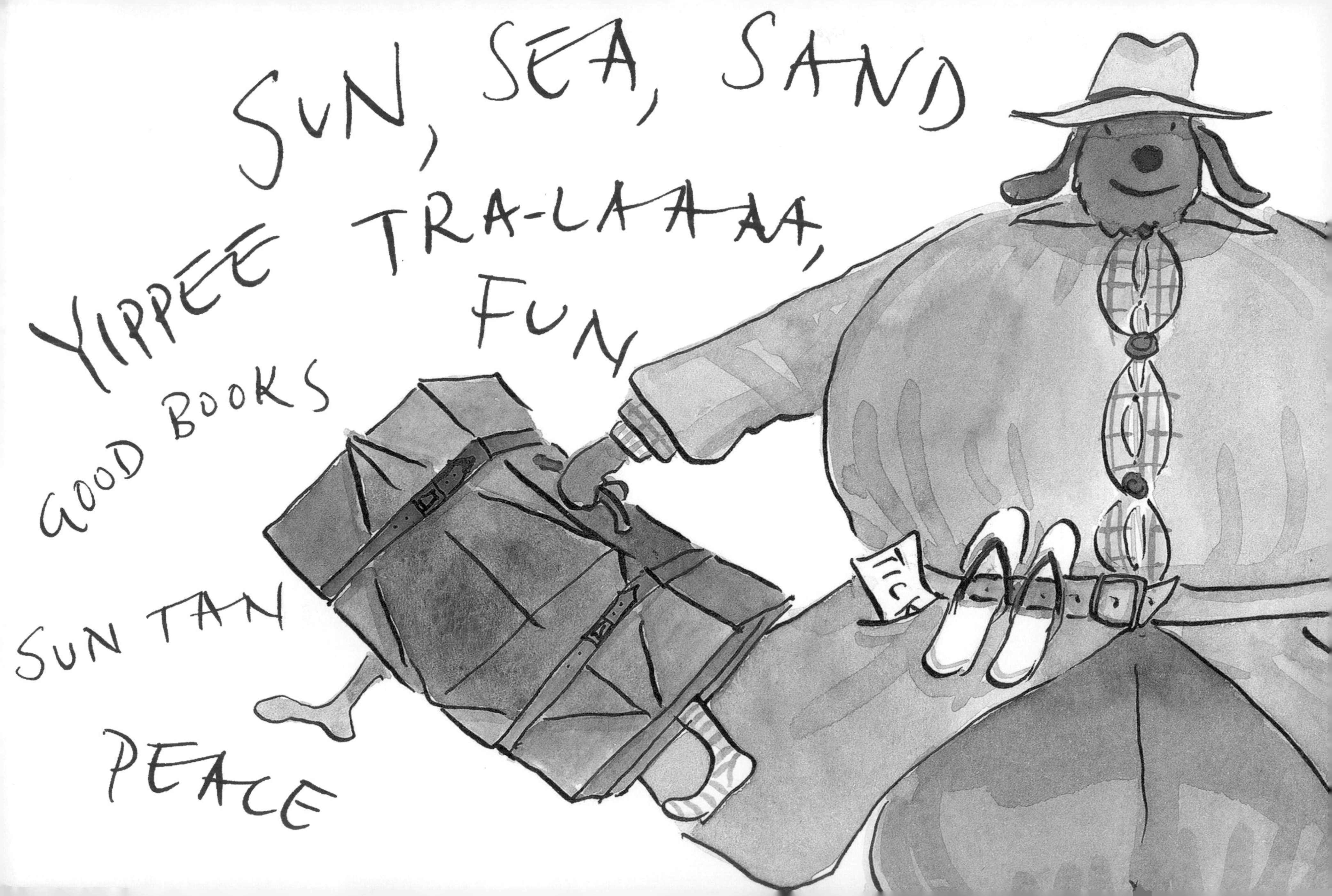
SUN, SEA, SAND
YIPPEE TRA-LAAAAA,
FUN,
GOOD BOOKS
SUN TAN
PEACE

HERE WE COME!
HOORAY
WAHOO!
ICE CREAM
HOLIDAYS FOREVER!
NEW FRIENDS
NEW THOUGHTS
NEW ME!

Wish you were here!
ARCHIE x